TREASURE NAP

TREASURE NAP

JUANITA HAVILL

ILLUSTRATED BY
ELIVIA SAVADIER

Houghton Mifflin Company
Boston 1992

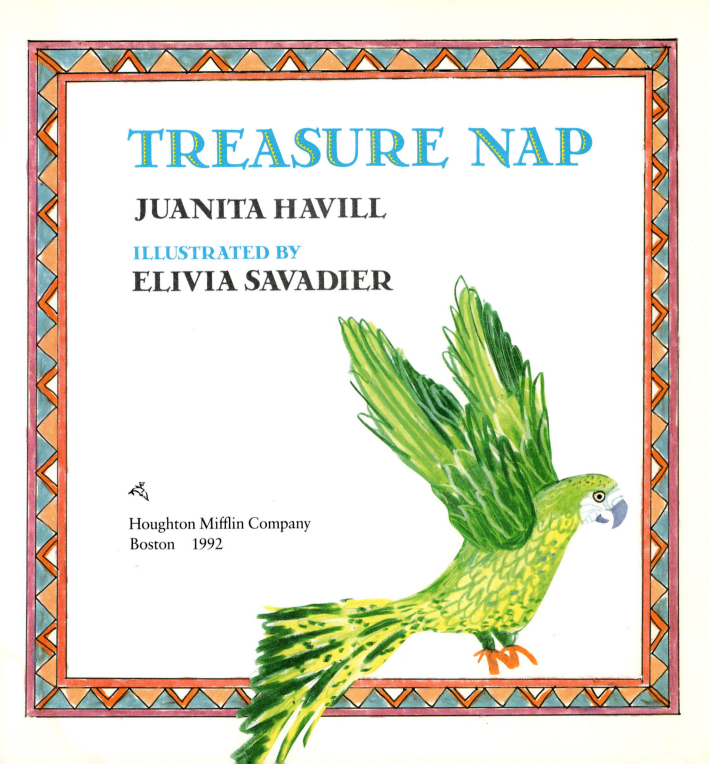

Library of Congress Cataloging-in-Publication Data

Havill, Juanita.
   Treasure nap / Juanita Havill ; illustrated by Elivia Savadier.
      p. cm.
   Summary: On an afternoon when it is too hot to sleep, a young girl
asks to hear the story about how her great-great-grandmother came to
the United States from Mexico, bringing a special treasure.
   ISBN 0-395-57817-5
   [1. Mexican Americans—Fiction. 2. Family—Fiction.]
I. Savadier, Elivia, ill. II. Title.
PZ7.H31115Tr   1992   91-28700
[E]—dc20   CIP
                   AC

Printed in the United States of America

HOR 10 9 8 7 6 5 4 3 2 1

For my mother.
And special thanks to Sandra Benítez,
who shared her travels with me.

—J.H.

For Alex and Laura.
Thank you for taking good care
of Sadye while I drew.

—E.S.

"It's too hot to take a nap, Mamá." Alicia got out of bed
and sat on the wicker trunk by the window.

6

"It's too hot to sew," Mamá said. She set her sewing
down and put the spools of thread back in a box.

7

Alicia slid off the trunk. "Can we open the trunk, Mamá, and take everything out?"

"It's too hot to open the trunk now," said Mamá. "Let's go downstairs where it's cooler."

Mamá got a big blue sheet from the linen closet and took fussy Ramón from his crib.

Alicia carried the pillows down the stairs all by herself.

Mamá flapped the sheet open and full so it billowed over Alicia's head like a sail.

The sheet puffed air in Alicia's face and settled to
the floor over her toes.

Alicia lay down on the wide blue sheet with Ramón.
She watched Mamá set the fan on the table behind a
bowl of ice cubes. The fan turned and hummed a breeze.

It felt as cool as water in a lake.

"Tell a story, Mamá," Alicia said. "Tell about the trip to the mountains."

Mamá smiled. "This is a story my mamá told me when it was too hot to sleep."

"Many years ago a little girl named Rita lived in a town in Mexico. Her papá sold canaries at the market. Her mamá wove baskets to sell. They worked hard, but they didn't earn enough for their family."

"One summer Rita went with her mamá and baby brother to visit her grandfather in his village in the mountains."

Alicia closed her eyes. She could see a little girl and her mamá and baby brother. And because she had heard the story before, she could see them walking beside icy mountain streams.

"The water gushed past them," Mamá said. "At night they slept in the shadows of pine trees."

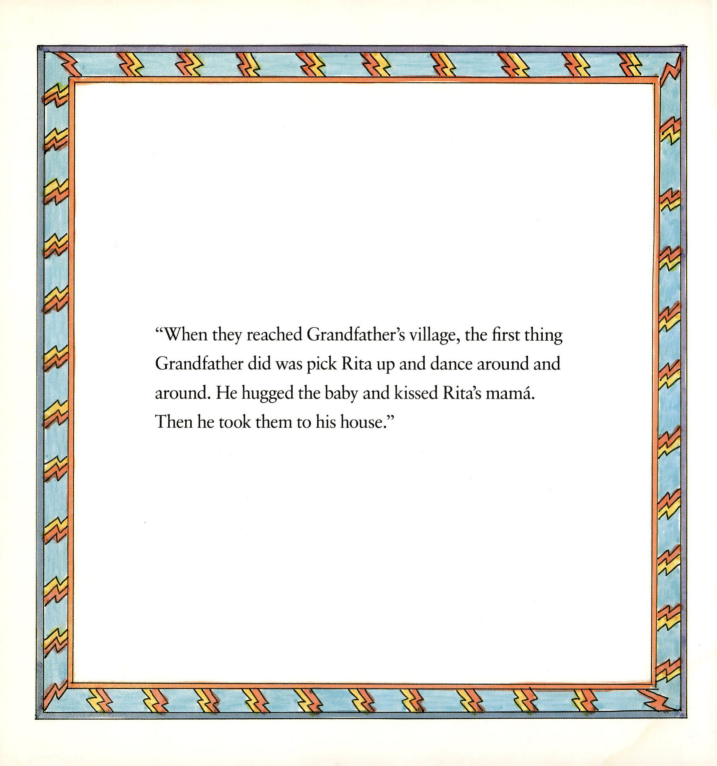

"When they reached Grandfather's village, the first thing Grandfather did was pick Rita up and dance around and around. He hugged the baby and kissed Rita's mamá. Then he took them to his house."

"It was dark inside, so he lit a lamp and set it on a wooden stool. The light flickered and made strange shadows on the wall.

"Rita saw stacks of wooden bird cages in one corner. She pointed to a thin tube hanging on the wall. 'What is that, Grandfather?' she said.

"'My *pito,*' he said. He took down the *pito* and played a song. It sounded like little birds chirping in the trees.

"Grandfather unrolled a mat on the floor for their bed. He gave them a serape as a cover."

"The next day Rita went into the forest with Grandfather. He showed her how to sit very still so that the birds flew near them."

"Later, he set her on his neighbor's burro and she rode round and round the village. On other days they made wooden bird cages. Grandfather even taught Rita how to play the *pito*."

"Rita didn't want to leave. She didn't want to say goodbye to Grandfather. But her mamá told her that is why they had come to the mountains in the first place—to say goodbye to Grandfather.

"Grandfather rolled up the serape and tied it for Rita to carry on her back. 'I wish I had a treasure to give you,' he said, and gave Rita a bird cage and his *pito*."

"Rita went back to her town with her mamá and baby brother. Then her papá brought them here to the United States to live."

"I know what happened next," said Alicia. "Rita grew up and she had Grandmother, and Grandmother grew up and she had you, and you grew up and you had me."

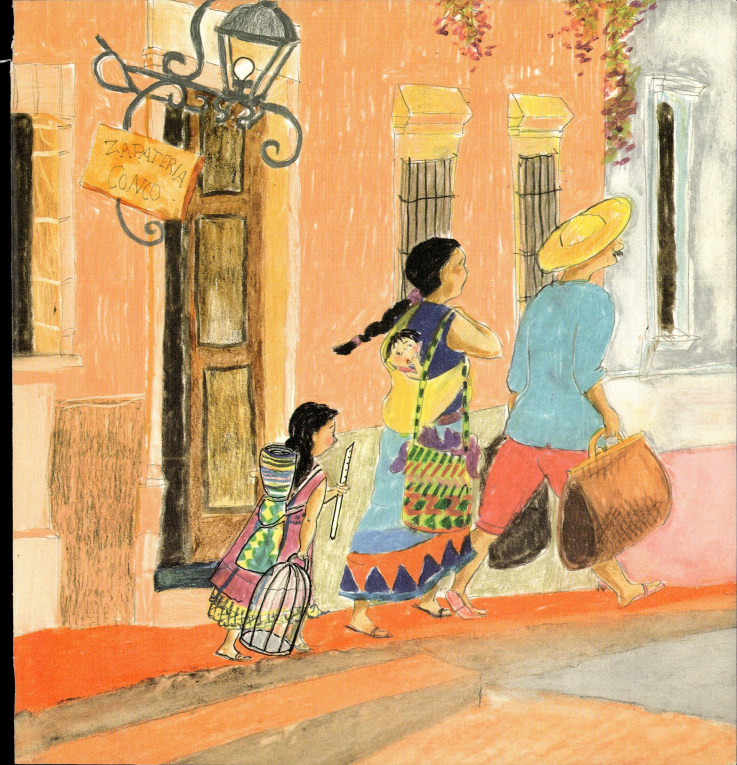

"Yes," said Mamá. "Rita came all the way to the United States to be your great-grandmother." She kissed Alicia on the forehead and Alicia fell asleep.

When Alicia woke, it was cooler. "Now can I open the trunk?" she asked.

"Yes," said Mamá, and they went upstairs.

Alicia opened the trunk. "Can I play with Great-Grandmother's treasure?"

"If you're careful," said Mamá. "It's your treasure, too."

Alicia took out the serape, the *pito,* and the wooden bird cage.
She closed the lid of the trunk and climbed on top.
Off she rode to the mountains. When she blew on the *pito,*
the birds came.

One bright green parrot flew right up to her and perched on top of the cage.